I0624591

MUD & DAISIES

Copyright © 2019 by Ynnek (Kenny) Bechtel

First Edition

Cover art by Rebecca Preble

ISBN 978-0-578-22121-2 (paperback)

www.storybunk.com

MUD & DAISIES

By Ynnek B

Cover Art: Rebecca Preble

SPECIAL THANKS TO:

LBC's Creative Writing Class: You all are why this little book exists! Thank you to everyone who helped me improve this story!

Pastor Jim: You are my great encouragement for writing! Thank you for pushing me to use the gifts that God has given me to make something beautiful.

MUD & DAISIES

There was a small family who lived in a tiny little house. The house sat right at the edge of the town, far up the road and near a lush green forest. The day started as any normal day might. "Shelby! Andrew! Wake up!" A voice echoed up the stairs towards closed doors. First came sounds of grumbling as the two strained to rise from their beds; then came the pitter patter of feet on the hardwood floor and, lastly, the quiet thumping of those little feet as the two children slowly marched down the stairs, rubbing their eyes.

"Mornin' Dad," Andrew said with a half-awake hand wave.

"Hi Daddy," Shelby added, sitting down at a table filled with lightly toasted bread and hot scrambled eggs. Immediately they began to pop pieces of the egg into their mouth one by one, each with a satisfied "mmm."

"What's the time Dad?" Andrew said, glancing from his plate to his father, who sat across from them.

"Eleven in the morning," he replied, shoving more eggs into his mouth in a hurried manner. "I'm a bit late today."

"But you only start work at twelve!" Shelby replied.

Their father took a big gulp from his glass of milk and then set it down empty. "I've been called into the shop early today, a few of the workers are..." he paused, unsure what to tell his children. Wrinkles covered his forehead. "They went missing," he said at last, rising from his chair and facing his head away from his children. His face went towards Shelby, who munched on her toast slowly in a worried manner.

"And I'll have to work late too, just for today, which means you'll have to make sure the outside lights are all on tonight. It gets dark at ten," he said, elevating his voice to a louder, faster, and seemingly anxious tone, "which means you'll have to make sure they are all on before then, or else..."

2

Andrew finished the sentence, "We'll go missing too."

His father looked at him with sorrow on his face, seeing his son's worrisome expression. "Yes," their father said sadly, sulking over to the window and picking up a picture. He looked at the picture. It was one of a smiling man in a pure white suit and a bright yellow tie. His head was resting on the head of another- a woman who wore a dress that was perhaps even more white, yet had yellow outlines running up and down her skirt. The two smiled, both holding an object and both with rings on their fingers. The object was yellow and white, a... The father put the picture down. It was a picture of himself, yet it didn't feel like it to him. Moving his hand to the right of the picture, he reached towards a vase with dying flowers. They were daisies - white peddled flowers with a yellow center. He lifted them out of the vase and sadly threw them in the trash.

"It'll be fine, Dad." Andrew said, putting his small fingers into his father's hand. "We'll be ok!"

His father looked at him and offered a small smile. Brightening his face, he lifted Andrew up and said, "Of course you will, because you are a brave little boy with a big heart! One just like your mother's."

"And you!" he said with another smile as he walked over to Shelby. "You are a responsible young lady, far more responsible than I ever could be!"

Shelby blushed as he offered her a kiss. "Oh, Daddy!"

He opened the door to leave. "Just remember," he said, turning back with a serious glance at the children. "Don't forget to turn on the lights, and, if you're hungry there is always food in the fridge. I'll be back at eleven. And Shelby," he added, pointing his finger, "you're in charge." Putting on his hat, he began to close the door, peeking his face through one last time. "Be good!" he said with a smile and walked off into the town.

...

After their father left, the two children washed the dishes and turned on the TV. After watching cartoons for a few hours,

Shelby decided that it was time to make lunch, and Andrew offered to help by setting the table.

"For lunch we will eat ham sandwiches with a side of grapes," Shelby said energetically. Andrew chose the desert. The two ate and then cleaned up the table the best they could.

Shelby looked at the clock. "It's two o'clock."

"Should we turn on the outside lights yet?" Andrew asked in reply.

"No," said Shelby. "Not until it is eight." So the two waited and waited as time ticked on. Time passed, and the two went outside to play frisbee, every so often looking towards the woods as if some monster could come from it at any minute.

"Is it eight yet?" Andrew asked worriedly, gazing into the dark forest beyond them.

"Six." Shelby replied.

Rain clouds began to roll overhead, so the two decided to go inside and eat dinner - another ham sandwich. Again, they ate and argued as all siblings do and eventually turned the TV back on. Time passed from six to six thirty, from six thirty to seven, from seven to eight. Time ticked on, from eight to nine, from nine...

"Nine thirty-five!" Shelby exclaimed with a gasp.

Andrew looked at her. "Daddy's gonna be mad at you!"

"Not if he doesn't find out," Shelby answered as she jumped from the sofa. With a whirl she ran off to the kitchen, reaching for the outside light. She flicked it. "There! All better."

But all was not better. As soon as the children turned to watch more TV, the lights flickered off!

"The lightning storms!" Shelby exclaimed, looking over her shoulder. The two children looked at each other and then rushed towards the kitchen once again.

Andrew watched as Shelby thumbed through drawers and cabinets. "What are you doing?"

"Dad set up a generator in the shed. I'm going to try to turn it on," Shelby replied.

"I wanna help you."

"No," Shelby whispered, peeking her head inside one of the cabinets. "It's too dangerous, and I am older than you."

"But I wanna help!" Andrew said louder, still standing in the same spot.

"Andrew," Shelby said, mimicking the 'calm voice' her father sometimes used when they were in trouble. "What if the big monsters come."

Andrew looked at his sister, who now was holding a flashlight. "I still want to come with you." His face turned pouty as he began to usher in his best fake cry. "Wahhh! Wahhh! I want to come with." His sister just looked at him narrowing her eyes. He continued to pout unceasingly. "Wahhhhhhh!"

"Oh, shut up already!" She said at last. "You can come, but we gotta do this quick."

Andrew, ceasing his exaggerated sorrow, smiled and walked out the door with his sister. It was now dark; they could see the other buildings brightly lit from a distance. They walked towards the shed, as their shoes crisply crunched the leaves beneath them. When they approached the shed, they twisted its metal handle.

"Shel," Andrew said with his voice shaking. "I don't think I should have come out here." More crunching sounds began, but this time it wasn't from them. There was some slithering, too. Andrew looked towards one of the trees and then to the bushes, which seemed to move! Swinging the shed door open, Shelby rushed in and promptly began to inspect the generator.

"Shel, work faster!"

Shelby ran her small fingers over the various switches, buttons, and wires. Her face squinted as she tried to remember how her father used to turn it on. "Everything is going to be okay, Andy," she said, half whimpering, trying to calm her little brother down. It wasn't working. Andy's face swung left and right as he looked towards the direction of the slithering sounds.

"I'm going inside," Andy whispered, as he turned to run for the door. Shelby turned as her brother began to move.

"Wait!" Shelby exclaimed, clenching her teeth. Andy didn't stop; his feet crunched through the leaves as he approached the door. But then, with an unsettling gurgle, the sound suddenly stopped. Shelby stood looking at the house in horror. Her mind filled with fear as a shadow grabbed her brother, and he disappeared.

"Andy!" she yelled. "Andy!" she yelled again louder. From the right she heard an unintelligible mumble. "Where are you?" She said as tears ran down her eyes. *It got him*, she thought, closing the shed door as she jumped in. Lightning flashed through the sky as she leaned her back against the small shed's wall. With an exhausted sigh she wiped mud from her face - mud that seemed to be dripping from the ceiling. She looked up, and with a scream everything went black.

...

The two woke up in a dark cavern; the walls twisted with slime and gook. It felt like blood was rushing towards their head, no, not blood... mud. Andrew wiggled around; both he and his sister were suspended upside down in cocoon-like bags with mud slowly creeping towards their faces. Andy tried to twist

9

free, but his attempt at escape failed. Shel woke up as well, to the same fearful fright her brother saw.

They were tall, slender creatures pacing back and forth, moaning and groaning, their feet lifting from the floor as they walked, making a slurping sound with every step. Wherever they went, a trail of mud followed (not that the kids could tell though, since the whole cavern was one mud-infested tunnel). Their fingers were long and droopy, as were their arms which reached down to their knees and seemed almost to hang limp as they walked. Their bodies were very similar, some smaller, some larger, some you could tell were either men or women, but others were harder to figure. All of them were covered in mud. But it was their faces that were perhaps the most horrifying. It seemed as if they had no face, save for the eyes which were eerie, small, mud tunnels that led to small, almost human-like, eyes that seemed to be glazed over.

Shelby let out a scream! One of the mud people turned its face towards her in an almost inhuman gesture and walked over to put its face near hers as if it were inspecting their recent catch. He lifted a finger to touch her nose and then moved it to the part of his own face where the mouth should have been. Putting one finger up, he tried to shush her. She let out another cry for help. The creature apathetically turned around and walked off.

"We're gonna die," Andrew said as the seemingly living mud drew towards his face.

"Let us go!" Shelby screamed in defiance. The mud people didn't listen; they just kept walking with their arms flopping at their sides. Zombie-like, cold, and mindless.

...

"Help us!" came a scream from a boy. "I don't want to die," the voice of a little girl echoed through the twisted mud tunnels. All the mud people kept walking; ignoring the desperate plea of the poor children.

One of the creatures turned her mud-pointed head to look towards the sound. The noise, it sounded like... Next came the cries. It was the kind of cry that one makes when he feels that all hope is lost. The creature knew what that meant. Transformation would be imminent. She reared her head back the way she had been walking.

Another cry of desperation echoed through the halls. And then, as if something clicked inside her brain (if she indeed still had one), she turned her head towards the echoing cavern. Quietly she mumbled to one of the passing mud men. The mud man grunted and continued walking. She was right. Her eyes widened with fear as she looked into the caves.

Unable to resist, she quickly lumbered through the muddied tunnels, bumping into mud men and mud women, none of them acknowledging her. She walked down twisting stairs and through black, swishing water, until she came to the cavern that held the helpless creatures. They were humans, small ones about the age of eight and nine. She knew what they were - children.

Without a word she twisted her head around, looking to see if anyone was watching, and then slowly approached the boy whose face was covered with mud. She stuck her hand on his muddied body and with a slurping sound began to draw the mud up towards her.

"Stop it!" the girl yelled. "Don't kill him!"

The mud lady looked slightly towards the girl but then refocused on the boy, sucking the mud cocoon with her hand. Slowly the mud receded from him until only his feet were connected to the cave's roof. She swiped at the string, letting the boy fall with a thud.

"I'm alright!" The boy said, energetically looking up towards the unexpected hero. "The Mud Lady saved me!"

Next, her head turned towards the girl, who still had tears in her eyes that were flowing down her upturned face. Taking her finger, the mud lady slid it across the girl's face, trying to catch the tear. It didn't work, of course, but rather made a long streak of mud above her eyebrows. The mud lady then did the same as she had done for the girl's brother, slurping up the mud until she was free as well. The tall creature stood hunching in the cave, looking at the two children who were now hugging each other and wiping the mud off the each other's face.

"Thank you," the girl said shyly. The mud lady nodded silently.

Once the sentiment ended, they were greeted with another noise. A deep, haunting moan bellowed through the cave, as a large mud man came with dripping hands. Others followed his lead. Stretching out her long arms and putting her hands out towards him, the lady tried to get him to stop. It seemed to work. The big blob of mud stopped in his tracks. Then, seeing the children behind her, he swung his arm, sending it crashing down towards her side. The thin mud woman flew across the room. Screaming, the children began to back away from the blob's stiffened hand as he reached for them to put them back into their cocoons. His arms got closer; he almost had them when the muddied heroine pounced on his back, putting her hands on top of his face and began pressing the mud over his eye holes to blind him. In desperation the blob tumbled back and forth, running into the rocky walls as he blindly tried to find his prey.

Seeing an opportunity, the mud lady ran towards the children and grabbed them both between her arms. She ran as fast as she could, speeding up the winding steps and past hoards of mud people until she reached a vine-filled area. Pushing aside the vines, she and the children entered a room that had a roof that seemed to leak pale goop.

"Quick sand!" the girl let out with a yelp. The mud woman looked at the girl and then at the boy. Looking up, she pointed one of her long fingers towards the roof.

"We can't make it through quick sand," the girl's voice echoed defiantly. The mud lady looked back to the vines as the other mud creatures eerily gurgled songs of doom. It was now or never.

...

Andrew didn't see it coming. The mud woman grabbed their shirt collars and with a jump sent them all up, flying into the quicksand. Or was it a jump? Perhaps her feet were still on

15

the ground, extending itself and pushing them all up through it; Andrew didn't know. All he knew was that this was crazy; a mud-covered creature was helping them! For what and why? He did not know.

The three of them slowly rose through the sand, feeling its weight tug down on them. But they made it, muddier than ever. The mud woman threw them away from the sand to pull herself out of it slowly. Standing at the edge of the pit, she let her arms droop and hunched over, as if almost to catch her breath.

"Who is this lady?" Andrew whispered to his sister.

"I don't know," Shelby replied. "but she seems different from the rest."

The mud lady stood up straight and turned around to look at them. But as she turned, a clawed hand emerged from the quicksand! The children let out a scream, and the mud lady flung her head around, widening her eyes. It wasn't just a hand; it was two hands. No, three! No, it was a whole host of hands and bodies rising from the sand. The mud lady turned, pulling the children by the hand, as she began to run through the lush green forest. To Andy's surprise the hand seemed gentle, yet still a bit slimy. Whenever a mud creature would get close to them, the children's new friend would pull them away.

"Over there!" Andrew yelled, spotting a field through the branches. Turning, they darted towards it as fast as they could. The grass tickled the children's legs. Not just grass... there was something else there. Whatever the case, it was good timing. The sun rose in the sky, and, to the children's surprise, the mud lady's hand began hardening; it was becoming dry and almost rock-like.

Andrew noticed it first. "Run faster!" he shouted. "The sun is coming up."

The mud lady began to heave, gasping for air as she reached for the shade at the other side of the pasture. She made it! Her muddied skin returned to its goopy normal texture. The three looked across the field from beneath the forest's shade, watching the other monsters flee from the heat of the sun. Andy and Shelby both took a deep breath, and soon enough both collapsed in exhaustion.

...

The sun shone brightly on the town as it rose, though few would have realized it. Another tragedy. According to the local news there was another kidnapping by those horrible beasts. This time they were children, and not just anyone's children - his children. He went into town and talked to the local police.

"I'm sorry, Kevin. We can have a search party out by twelve o'clock," an officer said. "We may be able to get a few neighbors to join us, but I wouldn't be so sure. Most of them are afraid of the woods, especially with all those hellish monsters around."

The children's father, Kevin, looked to the ground. "All I ask is that we look."

The officer sighed caringly, "We'll gather what we can."

Slowly, Kevin stood up from the officer's desk and walked outside, closing the door behind them. The walk to his house was long and tedious. Thoughts invaded his mind. He remembered the birth of his children and the smile of their mother at the sight of their chubby little faces. He remembered when they first learned how to walk and how to speak, and he remembered when those mud beasts took away their mother and how they were too young to really realize what they had lost. Now he had lost them. "I should have been there for them," he said, wiping a tear from his eye as he walked down the empty street. "I can't lose you," he mumbled to a person who wasn't there. "Not like I lost..." Reaching his house, he opened the door, crying as he went in.

...

Shelby never knew how much beauty could be in the forest. All her life she was told to stay away from it because "there's evil in there, evil beyond your comprehension!" At least that is what she was told by the townspeople. But what her father told her seemed to be more accurate, that the forest is a beautiful place that has been corrupted. There was so much beauty here that Shelby almost forgot everything that happened the night before.

Rising from the tree where she lay down to sleep with the shade of the branches hanging over her, she stood up, listening to the sounds of the birds chirping and watching a couple of playful squirrels run up and down the trees. *This is how it was supposed to be*, she thought.

Then, looking around, she saw the mud lady just sitting there at the edge of the woods, still covered by the shade, looking out to the field beyond. The field was filled with yellow and white.

"Those are daisies." Shelby said, cautiously approaching the silent lady. "They were my mommy's favorite flower. My daddy used to come out here to pick some for her." The mud woman's face looked towards Shelby's. "Sometimes my parents would pick them together." Shelby took the lady's muddy hand and began to pull. "Here, let's go pick some." The lady started to rise, but as soon as her hand reached the sunlight, she pulled it back again in pain.

"She can't go into the sun, Shel," Andrew's voice said from behind the two. "It hurts her." The mud lady's face looked back down to the ground as she sat, folding her arms over her knees. And then, Shelby had an idea.

"I know!" she said with glittering eyes. "Let's go pick some for her!" Andrew thought this was a grand idea, and the two ran around in the sun-lit field, as the mud woman watched them. Her eyes were filled with wonder or, perhaps, joy at the sight of the children playing in the field. When they were done, they came and gave four handfuls to the mud woman, who in turn held each flower to her eyes, studying them.

"Do you like them?" Andrew asked, with his arms behind his back. The mud lady nodded, with a few muddy drops coming from her eyes.

"You don't got much friends, do you?" Shelby asked, putting a hand on the silent woman's shoulder. "That's okay, cause we'll be friends."

"Yea!" Andrew replied gleefully. "We're friends!" Cheerfully, he put his hand out for a hand shake; the mud woman accepted it.

"My name's Andy," Andrew said, still shaking the mud woman's squishy hands. "And this is my sister Shel!" Shelby just waved, a gesture which the mud lady returned as well. "What's your name?" The mud lady only shrugged sorrowfully.

"She can't talk, remember?" Shelby blurted, looking her brother in the eye. "How about this," she continued, handing the mud lady another flower. "How about Daisy? Can we call you that?" The woman nodded.

"Then Daisy it is!" Andrew said, enthusiastically offering his hand again. "Nice to meet you, Daisy!" Daisy happily shook it again, letting out a silent laugh.

"Well," Shelby said, turning around looking at the field. "We better go. Daddy must be worried, and he said 'I'm in charge.'" But Daisy, with speed, rose to her feet and put her hands out.

"No," Shelby said sternly in reply. "Daddy is wondering where we are." Daisy's muddy face sank... literally. Then she lifted her head again, and using the palm of her hands she made a round shape out of mud, and tossed it into the field. The shape hardened.

"A ball!" Andrew said, running into the field to kick it.

"Fine," Shelby said concedingly, watching her brother. "But only for a little bit."

So the three kicked and threw and tossed the ball back and forth for some time. Daisy, of course, never left the shade of the trees.

Once again Shelby said, "We should be going now." But Daisy, widening her eyes like that of a hungry puppy, turned around, grabbed some of the flowers that they had given her, and twisted it into a crown. She placed the crown on Shelby's head.

"I'm not going to fall for your tricks, Daisy." In the end, Shelby fell for her tricks. The three of them played dress up, fastening leaves together with mud to make crowns, slimy little gloves, and capes. Shelby and Andrew even made Daisy a skirt

23

out of leaves. Then they made her a crown and cape and began dancing around her yelling, "All hail, Queen Daisy!" The kids laughed and maybe even Daisy, though it's hard to know. Because, again, they could see no mouth. The three kept playing all day and into the night. Soon darkness covered the land, and they knew it was time to go. For where there was darkness, mud monsters were soon to follow.

···

"Keep your flashlights up!" One of the officers said as he walked through the woods. Around them they heard sounds of crunching and crackling. Walking up to the quicksand pit, they stopped.

"There's no sight of them, Kevin," one of the officers said with a low tone. "We should return home." Kevin just looked sadly at the pit.

"Kevin," the officer continued. "We can return in the morning, but my men need sleep, and those creatures are swarming this place.

Kevin sighed, lowering his flashlight slightly, and said, "Let's go home."

The officers, a few neighbors, and Kevin sadly walked back. As they exited the woods, they began to hear crunching and crashing sounds, followed by inhuman moans and groans of lamentation and fury! Something cried from the distance. They heard another noise! A scream! A human scream! Suddenly the officers turned around, running at full speed as their flashlights waved through the night. Kevin followed closely behind. Hope and fear filled his brain. With a crash a large figure came lumbering out of the woods with others following close behind. The others, though, did not stay long. Upon seeing the bright rays of light coming from the officers' flashlights, they fled back into the woods, leaving only one remaining.

"Put the girl down!" An officer yelled, pointing his pistol at the tall creature's face. The creature obeyed, but the girl did not move from its side.

At this, Kevin burst through the crowd yelling. "Shelby!" His eyes were filled with excitement. "You're alive!" A smile of relief ran across her face as she lunged towards her father, embracing him.

"Sorry, Daddy. I forgot to turn on the light and then the electric…!"

Kevin rubbed the dirt off her head, muttering. "Its ok, its ok." over and over again. He then stood up, pointing a light at the mud woman. Her skin started to harden, and she began to back up slowly with fear in her eyes. But it wasn't the light that scared her. For she was looking around; she was looking for something… or someone.

"Where's Andy!?" Kevin asked thrusting the light towards her face. The officers surrounded Daisy, doing the same. The poor woman began to moan!

"You're hurting her!" Shelby yelled in anguish as Daisy's mud-slick skin began to harden.

"Where is he?" Kevin asked again as the white light illuminated his anger-filled face.

"Daddy!" Shelby cried out once again, weeping. "Don't hurt Daisy." She was now whimpering as her new friend was lying on the grass, slowly hardening into rock. Looking back at his daughter, uncertain what to do, Kevin stood up and turned off the light.

"Back up," he said to the officers. The officers hesitated, but did so.

"Can I trust you to rescue my son?"

Daisy nodded, as she pointed to the flashlight he held in his hand. Reluctantly he gave it to her, and without a word she sprinted back into the forest.

...

27

Daisy ran into the forest at full speed, crashing through trees and bushes until she reached the quicksand entrance. Jumping in, she hurried through the chambers, following the screams of Andrew. She had to make it in time. The confrontation with the officers held her back for a bit. But she was determined that she would save little Andy, even if it killed her. She ran through the catacomb-like tunnels until she reached the center.

Once again he was hanging from the ceiling upside down with mud covering his face. Behind him was a gigantic, muddied heart which thumped and thumped and thumped and thumped. As she approached the heart and the boy, she heard a low growl. Turning around, she saw the same blobby mud man that hit her a day before. He came lumbering towards her, except that this time he brought friends. A lot of friends, each of them moaning and groaning in an eerie chorus. Their minds were linked as one, all their minds except Daisy's, who by some odd coincidence had humanity snapped back into her when she first heard the children's screams.

She heard another scream. "Help! Daisy, Help!"

The mud men and women approached Daisy, each one of them pilling onto her and making a large bubble of icky goop. Daisy strained to escape, reaching one mucky arm through the bubble. Then another, and, finally, she pulled herself out of the goop making it to Andrew. But it was too late. As she stood, the mud rushed down Andrew's face and into his throat, as if to take control of him.

The mud bubble from which she had just escaped disappeared; now her foes were standing upright again and slowly walking towards her. In haste she turned, grabbed Andrew's cocoon, and pulled him from it, hoisting him over her shoulders. The army of mud didn't stop; it was time for her last resort. Reaching into her muddy side she pulled out the flashlight that Kevin gave her and pointed it to the heart. It wouldn't kill it, but it could do some damage. Bracing herself, she lit the flashlight and shown it directly at the heart. All of a sudden, the caverns walls started to shake as if the dead were being raised.

Shouts of agony went up as the heart convulsed, causing the mud people to scream in pain.

The screams were horrifying, and they felt horrifying, too. Daisy felt as if some deadly virus were at war within her. Andy shook with pain. Daisy let out a scream, falling to the floor. Wincing with her eyes as the mud on her body shook, she pushed herself back up and began to run. She ran through the tunnels and up the quicksand, pain searing through her body until she reached the edge of the woods. Only then the pain stopped, and all was quiet.

Kevin and Shelby were waiting there. The sun was starting to come up, but Daisy endured the heat.

"He's dead." Kevin replied with a cry, seeing his son covered with mud. Daisy looked at him and put a hand on his shoulder, only to move it back to his son. Much like before, Daisy stuck her hand over Andrew's face.

Kevin began to reach for her arm, but Shelby grabbed it, saying, "Wait, it'll be okay."

The sun came closer. Daisy closed her eyes and with all her strength sucked the mud that was filling his lungs up into herself. After a minute she removed her hand and pointed to a bottle of water at their father's side. The father opened the bottle and poured it into his son's mouth. After a few moments of silence, he began to cough and then breath.

Opening his eyes, he jumped up and hugged Daisy. Shelby did too. And then so did their dad.

"Thank you." he said, quietly looking up at her. "Thank you for everything." Her head was far above his. She looked down at him as he looked up. Daisy then reached into her side, pulling a muddied flower from it, doing her best to brush off the mud. She handed it to the children's father. Kevin stared at the muddied flower; it had a yellow center with white petals. It was a daisy. The sun began to rise in the sky, and Daisy began to leave. Waving, she turned around and walked back into the forest without saying a word.

...

The town rejoiced as Andrew and Shelby returned with their father. Andy, having been half-conscious of the events that transpired, told the officers about the mud people as well as the heart within their tunnels. The town asked questions, and the kids told them about the strange mud lady whom they named Daisy and how she rescued them when all hope was lost. While the kids told the town everything, their father was quiet and returned to home. Later that night after they all had showered and after the lights were lit their Father walked outside again.

"Daddy?" Andy asked. "What are you doing?"

He had an empty vase in his hand, as well as the dirty daisy their mud friend had given them. He reached for the hose and turned it on, partially filling a bucket.

"Do you think we'll ever see Daisy again?" This time it was Shelby who asked the question.

Their father smiled. "I wouldn't be surprised," he said, lightly dipping the daisy into the water and gently washing away the dirt. Andy and Shel sat next to him, putting their heads on each of his shoulders.

"It's a beautiful thing, kids," he said as he pulled the dripping, now clean daisy from the bucket. "There's really no mud that can't be washed away." The three of them stood up and walked into the house. "I'm glad we're all together," the father said. "I'm glad we're *all* together."

Looking to the hills, he closed the doors. There, far in the distance, a muddy figure stood. Daisy's eyes glistened joyfully with hope and happiness as she turned, walking back into the wood

ABOUT THE AUTHOR:

Hi! I'm Kenny! But you can call me Ynnek! Pen names are fun!

As a child I always was a storyteller, whether I was imagining myself as a spectacular superhero or filling in the blanks between each *Star Wars* movie, my mind always was always ready to explore new stories. I remember jotting down idea after idea in High School and it seems that I've never really stopped even in college.

Currently I am studying Pastoral Ministry at Lancaster Bible College but when I am not preaching the Bible you can typically find me reading, watching, and often writing stories that I find entertaining. The story you are reading now is just one example of the stories running around my head. They may be MY stories, but they are OUR entertainment. I hope you enjoyed this story as much as I do!

If you want to follow my writing escapades or contact me, visit my blog at storybunk.com! See ya there!

www.ingramcontent.com/pod-product-compliance
Lightning Source LLC
Chambersburg PA
CBHW050916120626
46552CB00004B/1610